Mischief and Mayhem!

*Look out for more stories
about Disastrous Dez!*

Spooks and Scares!

Mischief and Mayhem!

Mary Hooper

illustrated by Judy Brown

SCHOLASTIC

Scholastic Children's Books,
Commonwealth House, 1-19 New Oxford Street,
London, WC1A 1NU, UK
a division of Scholastic Ltd
London ~ New York ~ Toronto ~ Sydney ~ Auckland
Mexico City ~ New Delhi ~ Hong Kong

First published by Scholastic Ltd, 2002

Text copyright © Mary Hooper, 2002
Illustrations copyright © Judy Brown, 2002

ISBN 0 439 99450 0

Printed and bound in Great Britain by Cox & Wyman Ltd, Reading, Berkshire

2 4 6 8 10 9 7 5 3 1

Chapter One

"Oh no!" I heard Dad groan from the phone in the hall. And then he changed his tone a bit and said, "Don't worry. You can't help it, can you? Thanks for letting me know, Mrs Keynes. Hope you feel better tomorrow."

He crashed the phone down. "Blast the woman!" he said. "Getting flu today, of all days. What a nuisance."

It was October and the first day of half-term. I got up from my PlayStation and put my head round the sitting-room door. "What's up?"

"Mrs Keynes can't have you today, that's what's up. She's got flu." Dad looked at me suspiciously. "Dez, what did you do last time you were over there? Did you get those goldfish out again?"

I shook my head. "Course not! I only did it once. And that was *years* ago."

"No, it was last July," Dad said. "On the first day of the holidays." He looked at me and sighed. "There's nothing else for it. I'll have to take you in with me."

"Cool!" I said. I liked going to work with Dad. He was manager of the sports department at O'Connors, a big store in town. The last time I'd gone in with him I'd made a camp in the stockroom. Then I'd inflated a camping bed, put up a tent, tried on some sports shoes (miles too big), broken a pair of swimming goggles and nearly given an old lady a heart attack by lying under a pile of sleeping bags and making noises like a bear.

The women who worked there had all made a fuss of me and bought me chocolate bars, and the men had all played on my PlayStation.

"Yeah, cool..." Dad echoed. But not in the same sort of way as I'd said it, though.

He clapped his hands. "You'd better get ready then, matey!" He looked at his watch. "Get out of those pyjamas and find something decent to wear. We leave in exactly three and a half minutes."

I bounded upstairs to my bedroom where my clothes were heaped at the end of my bed in a pile as large as a volcano. I burrowed into it, flinging things backwards over my head until there was another, smaller, volcano on the other side of the room.

Almost at the bottom, I found my best blue T-shirt – it was quite clean apart from a yellow mark from where we'd had scrambled egg a few nights back.

I put it on, thinking that
volcanoes of clothes are
much better to find things
in than chests of
drawers. With chests
of drawers, everything
has to be neat and flat, but with volcanoes
it all goes in a nice jumbled heap.

"Ready?" Dad bellowed up the stairs.

"Nearly!" I stood on the bed
and leaped into my jeans,
which were new and
still standing, stiff
and upright, where
I'd jumped out of them
the night before.

I dashed into the bathroom, put a bit of toothpaste on my finger and squished it over my teeth, then swung down the stairs three at a time.

Dad looked me up and down. "What's that on your T-shirt?"

"Egg," I said.

"Egg and fresh minty toothpaste." He sighed. "Oh well, I suppose you'll do."

He lifted up his sports bag. "I've got your PlayStation, two books and an old comic. Okay?"

"Sure," I said. "But I won't need all that. I'm going to be helping you."

"In your dreams," he said. He narrowed his eyes at me. "You're going to be sitting quietly in the stockroom, unseen, unheard and undreamed of. Okay?"

"Okay," I said meekly.

Chapter Two

When we arrived at O'Connors it wasn't open for customers and I felt quite important going with Dad through the side doors and straight up into the staff canteen, where we had cornflakes and toast and Marmite.

When I'd eaten enough (well, what *Dad* said was enough), we went downstairs to the sports department and he put me in the stockroom, which was a long narrow room with loads of shelves containing sports gear in crates and boxes and bundles.

While I was sitting there, looking around and thinking about what I was going to do first, Mrs Ellis came in to admire me.

"Well, haven't you grown!" she said. Mrs Ellis was Dad's second in command and she was small and round. She wore a beige suit and had beige fluffy hair to match. All she needed was a red bow round her neck and she'd have looked like a human teddy bear.

She pretended to feel my muscles. "My! Aren't you doing well. Your dad's certainly feeding you right!"

This wasn't what I liked to hear. If people thought I was being fed well, then I didn't get bought any sweets. I shrank down a little and sucked my cheeks in, trying to look thin.

"Had your breakfast, have you?"

"I've had *some* breakfast," I said. "Dad took me to the canteen."

"I can see that. Did you enjoy your cereal?"

"How did you..."

"You've got milk all along your top lip and a couple of cornflakes stuck to your T-shirt," said Mrs Ellis, and she winked at me, grabbed my comic and took it away to read behind the counter.

Left on my own in the stockroom, I carried on studying the shelves. There were tennis rackets, boxes of golf balls, spiked shoes, head bands, shuttlecocks and training vests on one lot of shelves.

And cycling gear, golf umbrellas, squash rackets, eye shields and padded socks on the other. Masses of stuff just waiting to be investigated...

I peered out. The door was open but there was a green curtain over the doorway so that the customers couldn't see in. Dad was on the other side of the department, chatting to two men – his under-managers. His words came back to me, "Don't, under any circumstances, touch the stock, Dez. There were several things damaged last time you were here. Just remember, if things get spoiled they can't be sold."

I glanced at my PlayStation. I hadn't bothered to switch it on, yet. Well, there were so many other things around that could be played with.

*If things get spoiled
they can't be sold.*

I sighed longingly.

I looked at the box of shuttlecocks. I remembered them from last time: when you threw them into the air they always came down head first. Like parachutes. You could have races with them: right hand against left hand.

*If things get spoiled
they can't be sold.*

So I'd better not.

I sat on my hands, turned away from the shuttlecocks and saw the squash rackets.

Once, my friend James had gone to sleep on a racket and had woken up with criss-cross lines all over his face. He told me he and his mum had played crosswords on it.

How long would it take, I wondered, to get criss-cross lines all over my face?

It wouldn't hurt to just look at a squash racket, would it?

Or to throw a few shuttlecocks up in the air, very lightly and gently?

Before I knew it, I was up and into the boxes. I pulled the shuttlecocks out of their plastic wrapping and threw them into the air.

And then I got hold of a squash racket and pushed it hard against my face. I'd play races with the shuttlecocks and find out which was fastest. And while I was racing them, I'd be squishing my face on to the squared strings of the racket. And then I'd...

The curtain was suddenly pulled aside and I nearly jumped out of my skin. Six shuttlecocks fell to the floor all around me.

"Excuse me, young man," came a deep voice. It wasn't my dad, it was an older man wearing a brown suit and a red bow tie.

I gulped. Was this the boss – Mr Trotter? Dad had told me before that he sometimes came down from head office on surprise visits.

"I was just … er … squishing and er … squashing…" I mumbled apologetically. "Seeing which shuttlecock reached the ground first. I know if things are spoiled they can't be sold – but I wasn't hurting them."

The man looked a bit twitchy, and started fiddling with his bow tie, but he didn't seem to be bothered about the shuttlecocks. "Is the manager around?" he asked.

"That's my dad," I said proudly. "He's over the other side of the department talking to his men. I'll get him, shall I?"

Mr Red Bow Tie shook his head. "No need. I've come from ... er ... head office. I've just got to collect some squash rackets."

"Sure!" I said. "Which ones?"

"All of them," the man said. He produced two huge nylon bags. "As many as will fit in here."

"They're up there," I said, pointing. "I'll help you."

The man glanced outside, looking up and down the department. "Quick as you can, then, sonny," he said.

Chapter Three

Dad and I stared at each other.

He had the same sort of look on his face as when I'd once put a whole egg in the oven to cook, and it had exploded. "You did what?" he said. "You gave all the squash rackets to…" He covered his face with his hands and made an "Eee-aarrgghh" sort of noise.

And it was only then that I realized. "Oh," I said. "You mean he wasn't…"

There was a long silence, then Dad did the "Eee-aarrgghh!" noise again. Then he went straight out of the stockroom and started calling to people, and ringing them up, and waving his hands about and stuff.

I watched him for a while, and then I went and sat very quietly and neatly with my hands folded in my lap.

After a moment Mrs Ellis came in. I hung my head and looked sorry for myself.

"Now, I've told your dad it's no good going on at you," she said in her soft, teddy-bearish voice. "We've had things like this happen before. Thieves. Tricksters. Con-men. It's just bad luck that one should come along when you were in the stockroom."

I made a forlorn little noise.

"It was probably an awful shock for you."

"Awful," I said in a low voice. "Thieves and tricksters. I tried to stop them..."

"Of course you did!" she said. "Now, let's get you out of the stockroom where we can keep our eye on you. How about coming on to the shop floor with me? You can sit behind the counter and sort out the carrier bags."

"That sounds exciting," I said.

"Well, I don't know about *that*," she said, missing my sarcastic tone. "But it'll keep you out of mischief."

"OK," I muttered, "but I'm really hungry." I tried to suck my cheeks in again. "Is it time for elevenses?"

She looked at her watch.

"It's not even ten o'clock yet. But I daresay we can go up to the canteen and get you a little snack. And hopefully, by the time we come back your dad will have calmed down."

When we returned from the canteen, a small amount of hot chocolate and a few crumbs of digestive biscuit had joined the egg, cornflake and toothpaste on my T-shirt. I thought it looked quite good. Like one of those modern-art pictures that you can't make out which way up they're supposed to be.

Dad *had* calmed down a bit. "I've phoned head office and it looks as if we'll be able to claim most of it back on the shop's insurance," he said to Mrs Ellis. He narrowed his eyes at me. "But Dez – you watch out, right? If someone else comes along pretending to be from head office, let me or someone else know before you let them help themselves to our rackets, right?"

"Right," I said.

He looked at my T-shirt and tutted. "Is there something from old stock you can put on him, Mrs Ellis? He looks like a walking advertisement for the canteen."

"I'll see what I can find," she said.

Dad went off to see someone about golf balls and Mrs Ellis got me a tennis shirt – one of those ones with the three buttons and collar. It said **ANYONE FOR** on the front, and **TENNIS?** on the back. I put it on over my blue one and it came down to my knees, but Mrs Ellis said it looked okay.

By then it was quite busy in the department. Mrs Ellis went off to show some customers the running machines and left me sitting on the floor behind the counter with a jumbled heap of bags which I was supposed to sort into neat piles. The bags were made of thick white paper, all different sizes, and had O'CONNORS written on them in big green letters.

I started sorting. There were five different sizes, all muddled up, but it didn't take very long to sort them out.

I sat there and frowned at them. Why were paper bags always so boring? Why didn't they have pictures on them? They could have comic-strip characters, and dragons, monsters and dinosaurs.

Hmm... It would take me ages to do dragons, but ... but I could draw something inside the three Os in O'CONNORS. I could make them into little faces...

In a tray behind the counter I found a thick felt-tip pen. I experimented with the Os, making first of all a cat's face, then a rabbit's face, then a tiger's face, trying to decide which was best.

After this I did a pig's face, with a little curly tail on the top of the O. It looked brilliant. So good, in fact, that I decided that every single O on every bag should be a pig.

Chapter Four

Carefully, I began to work my way through the bags. I started with the big bags and went down to the small ones. These were so small that you couldn't see clearly what I'd drawn, so I wrote "pig's face" underneath, with an arrow pointing towards it. Just to be clear.

When I was on the last one, Mrs Ellis came back.

"How are you getting on, Dez?" she asked, smiling at me over the counter, and then she saw the bags and gave a shriek. "What are you *doing*?"

"Making the bags look more interesting," I said.

"Dogs' faces..." she said in a stunned voice.

"Pigs!" I pointed at the word on the smaller bags. "See. It says so here."

"Ohmygoodness," she said faintly. "What on earth will your father say?"

"'Spect he'll be pleased," I said, standing up behind the counter. "He likes art."

Mrs Ellis stood there as if turned to stone, gazing in admiration at my bags. Suddenly, I heard a shout of "Hey, Dez!" from the other side of the department. I looked over and saw my friend, Sasha Smith, standing by the golf trollies with her mum.

"It's my friend from school," I said to Mrs Ellis.

Mrs Ellis seemed to snap out of her trance. "Run along and talk to her, then," she said.

I felt a bit embarrassed going over there in the **ANYONE FOR** T-shirt because it looked a bit as if I was wearing a mini-dress, but Sasha didn't mention it. Her mum looked at me a bit funny, though.

"What are you doing here?" Sasha asked. She was bouncing a netball up and down and I looked at her severely.

"If things get spoiled they can't be sold," I said.

"What are you doing here?" she asked again, still bouncing. "Are you buying something?"

I shook my head importantly. "I'm working," I said. "Holiday job."

"Holiday job?" her mum said sharply. "Surely not. Children aren't allowed to work in a shop until they're fifteen."

I shrugged and decided to change my story. "Well, sort-of working," I said. "I'm doing artwork and stuff. Designing things."

Sasha looked at me admiringly. "Yeah? Cool."

Her mother looked at me, too. But her look was one of the eyebrows-raised, I-don't-believe-a-word-you're-saying type looks.

"I've just designed some new carrier bags," I said.

Sasha's mum tugged at her arm. "Come along, Sash. I want to try the sports shop in the high street." She nodded towards the golf equipment. "The price of these trollies is exorbitant!"

I wasn't sure what this meant so I nodded enthusiastically. "Yes," I said. "Most people say that."

Sasha was frowning at me. "Do you *really* work here?" she asked.

I crossed my fingers. "Course I do."

"Prove it." She pointed towards a woman standing by a rail of sports clothes. "Go and serve that woman over there."

"Okay!" I said. I went over. The woman was very large and seemed to get larger the closer I got. By the time I was standing next to her she was roughly the size of a small block of flats.

"Ahem," I coughed politely, looking up and marvelling at her size.

The woman turned. "Yes?"

"Can I help you, modom?"

"I doubt it," she said, looking at me as if I were something nasty on the bottom of her shoe. "I'd like to see a proper assistant."

"I am a proper assistant," I said, and added, "sort of," in a quieter voice.

She stared at me again. "I've heard of shops being short-staffed but I didn't know they were recruiting from nursery school."

I gave her my glowering, icy look, guaranteed to kill at fifty paces.

"Oh, very well," she said after a moment. She pointed to something on the rail. "Do you do this navy blue tracksuit in my size?"

I looked her up and down. "I should hardly think so," I said. "But we do have navy blue tents."

There was a moment's silence as she took this in. "What?" she said. "*What? What!*" Each time she spoke, she seemed to puff herself up, growing upwards and outwards like an Incredible Growing Woman. "How *dare* you!"

I was about to make a break for it, jump into the lift and get away, when I heard Dad's voice. *"Pigs!* Where is he now?" Then he said, "Oh no, he's talking to a customer. Dez!" he called. "Come here straight away, please. *Now!"*

"Excuse me ... duty calls..." I said graciously to the Incredible Growing Woman. I went over to Dad.

"What are these pigs doing on these bags?" Dad asked sternly.

I looked. "Not a lot," I said. "Just sitting there like pigs do. I could make them more varied if you like. I could put them on little chairs or have them poking their heads out of their sties or..."

"That's enough," he said. "You know what I mean. We shouldn't have pigs on our carrier bags. It's not businesslike."

"But it's more interesting," I said.

"That's as may be, but our Managing Director, don't forget, is called Mr Trotter."

I put two and two together. "Ooops!" I said.

"Yes, quite," said Dad.

"Excuse me!" The Incredible Growing Woman had appeared behind us. "That ... that child there," she boomed. "To whom does that child belong? I have never been so insulted in..."

Before she could say another word Mrs Ellis came to my rescue. She swept me along behind the counter shouting, "Come along! Time for our lunch!"

Whipping off my **ANYONE FOR** T-shirt, she pushed me towards the stairs. "See you all later!"

Chapter Five

When we came down from lunch, Dad was still slightly fuming.

"What did you say to that customer?" was the first thing he asked. "She said you'd been terribly rude to her. Something about a tent..."

I gave him my innocent, unblinking look. "I just told her where the tents were," I said.

"Did she *ask* where the tents were?" Dad said, looking at me suspiciously.

"Not exactly..."

"I see. Dez, I think we need to have a serious talk."

Mrs Ellis looked at us with round, brown teddy-like eyes. "He was only helping," she said. "Poor little lad. I'm sure he didn't mean to cause any trouble."

I tried to shrink, become thin and neglected. This was quite difficult, seeing as I'd just eaten a tuna sandwich, a ham roll, a slice of pizza and two slabs of fruit cake and my tummy had expanded my best blue T-shirt to stretching point. Looking down at it, I noticed that the modern-art display had now been joined by some tomato pips, a trail of tuna mayo and a couple of sultanas.

Dad turned to Mrs Ellis. "Yes, thank you for your input, Mrs Ellis," he said. "But 'poor little lad' is not quite how I'd describe him. He looks to me more like a hamster who's been stocking up for hibernation."

"Hamsters don't..." I began, but stopped as Dad gave me a heavy look.

"D'you want me to keep my eye on him for the rest of the afternoon?" Mrs Ellis asked quickly.

"I want you to tie him up with rope, put a gag in his mouth, a paper bag over his head and sit on him," Dad said heatedly. "That's what I *want*. But failing that, yes – please keep your eye on him for the rest of the afternoon." And he went off, wiping his brow with his hanky.

"Now," said Mrs Ellis, "I think we'd better put that tennis T-shirt back on you. Your own one looks a tiny bit mucky."

"Does it?" I said, looking surprised. "Dad washed it last February and it's due to be washed again in November." A look of absolute horror crossed her face.

"Only joking!" I said, grinning.

She put the **ANYONE FOR** T-shirt over my head.

"You must stay in the stockroom from now on. Get your books, and your comic and your PlayStation, and keep out of the way of the customers."

"What about afternoon tea?" I asked.

"Not a minute before three o'clock," she said firmly. "And don't come out. I'll come and get you."

I stayed in there for *hours.* I played the game with the shuttlecocks, and squished my face on the squash rackets, and read my books, but when I looked at my watch only twenty-four minutes had gone by.

I turned on my PlayStation and played a couple of games, then Dad came back from the canteen and it started to get busy in the department. I watched round the door as customers came and went, tried out golf clubs, swung tennis rackets and lifted weights up and down above their heads.

It was then, when the shop floor was at its busiest, that I saw a man acting very strangely. He was shortish, about the same age as Dad, wearing a navy blue blazer, and he kept dodging around the back of the big stand which contained the footballs.

His eyes were everywhere. First he was watching Dad, then he was watching Mrs Ellis and the others as if – *it suddenly came to me* – as if he was planning something. As if he was making sure they were out of the way so he could get up to No Good. Just like Mr Red Bow Tie had done this morning.

But he hadn't reckoned on me being there. He was watching them. But I was watching *him*. Daylight robbery! I wasn't going to let anyone get away with it again.

Chapter Six

First of all I tried to attract Dad's attention by coming out of the stockroom and waving at him. He didn't take any notice of this, so I went over and tugged at his sleeve. Unfortunately I tugged just when he was demonstrating a golf swing to a customer, and the club came back sharply and cracked the customer on the shin.

Dad – and the customer – weren't too pleased.

"What are you doing? Go away!" Dad said to me as he picked up the customer. He was speaking out of the corner of his mouth so I could hardly hear him.

"There's a man…" I began.

"Away. Get back!" Dad muttered, then very quietly, "Pretend you don't belong to me."

"But he's a robber…"

"Rubbish!" He raised his voice slightly, "What are you doing here, young man?"

"I came in with you this…"

"Off you go. Can't you see what you've done?" With his eyes rolling dreadfully, Dad pointed me back towards the stockroom. "Off you go at once."

"But…"

"OFF WITH YOU!"

So I offed.

I went back to the stockroom and peered at the robber from behind the curtain. He was pretending to be looking at a rail of tracksuits by then. Every so often, though, he'd glance over at one of the staff to make sure they hadn't spotted him.

He began to walk towards me and as he did so, every detective story I'd ever read raced through my head. Here was my chance! My chance to catch a real thief, to make it up to Dad for Mr Bow Tie, to receive the grateful thanks of everyone in the store and to be allowed to eat everything I wanted from the canteen...

I didn't want him to know that I'd already spotted him, so as he drew nearer I pretended to be studying the green curtain. "There's a very rare fly crawling up this curtain," I said chattily.

"Young man," he said, "I don't know who you are but I'm from head office..."

I nearly burst out laughing but, like a true professional, I kept my cool. "Oh yes?" I said. "And I suppose you've come to collect a couple of bags of squash rackets?"

"No," he said. "I've come to collect some diving watches."

"I thought so," I said. "Come right in! I'll get them for you."

"I don't think..."

"Come on! I've got them right here in the stockroom!"

Beckoning madly, I got the man into the doorway. I then whisked round, gave him a shove from behind, slammed the door and turned the key in the lock.

"Let me out!" he shouted.

"No!" I said. "I'm going to get my dad and the police and they'll take you away and lock you up for good!"

I sprinted across the shop and tugged at
Dad's arm. Luckily, this time it didn't have a
golf club on the end of it. "Quick! I've
caught a robber!" I puffed. "He's locked in
the stockroom."

"Don't be silly," Dad said.

"I have! I have! He wanted to steal the
diving watches!"

"Don't be so..." Dad began, then he said.
"What?"

"A robber," I said. "He's in the stockroom.
Call the police!"

By now, there was a lot of shouting coming from the stockroom. It was mainly along the lines of "Let me out!" but there were also quite a few swear words.

Dad picked up his phone, looking shaken. "I don't believe it!" he said. "Not two in one day! I'll get the security men."

Within minutes, two big huge security men arrived. They, Dad and the two under-managers stood in front of the stockroom door while I sat on the counter next to Mrs Ellis, forced to watch from a distance.

More pounding and shouting came from behind the door as one of the men turned the key.

Desperate for a piece of the action,
I slipped away from Mrs Ellis to get a closer
look. The door was opened.

"Grab him!" I shouted. "Don't let him get
away!"

"Got you!" Dad shouted, "Got you ... er
... Mr Trotter, sir."

I shrank back. *Mr Trotter!* Dad's boss...

Chapter Seven

"So how come this young lad isn't at school?" Mr Trotter asked Dad a few minutes later. The security men had disappeared, the under-managers were back serving customers and we three: Mr Trotter, Dad and me, were in the stockroom.

The two of them had been talking about the earlier Great Racket Robbery (but not my part in it) and – lo and behold! – it turned out that Mr Trotter was actually pleased with me, *thrilled* that someone in the department was on the ball.

It also turned out that – now that he was out – he hadn't minded being locked in the stockroom. That it was what he would want to happen to someone who was trying to rob his store.

"Dez is only here today because it was an emergency," Dad said. "It's half-term and the child-minder couldn't have him." He coughed nervously. "He'll go to his gran's tomorrow. You can rest assured it won't happen again, sir."

Mr Trotter put an arm round my shoulder. "Don't worry about it!" he said chirpily. "You've got yourself a very enterprising lad here. I realize he's too young to be on the shop floor now, but as soon as he's fifteen I want him to have a Saturday job in this department. Saturdays and school holidays. Okay, youngster?"

I beamed at him. "Yeah! Cool!" I said.

Dad coughed uneasily. "Yes ... er ... cool," he repeated.

But not in quite the same way as I'd said it...